P9-DUF-606

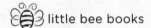 little bee books

An imprint of Bonnier Publishing USA
251 Park Avenue South, New York, NY 10010
Copyright © 2017 by Bonnier Publishing USA
All rights reserved, including the right of reproduction in whole or in part in any form. LITTLE BEE BOOKS is a trademark of Bonnier Publishing USA, and associated colophon is a trademark of Bonnier Publishing USA.

Library of Congress Cataloging-in-Publication Data:
Names: Kent, Jaden, author. | Bodnaruk, Iryna, illustrator.
Title: Attack of the stinky fish monster! / by Jaden Kent; illustrated by Iryna Bodnaruk.
Description: First edition. | New York: Little Bee Books, [2017] | Series: Ella and Owen; #2 |
Summary: Ella and her twin brother Owen head out on a new adventure in search of special ingredients to make their mom a cake, but end up being turned into newts, and running into a Stinky Fish Monster that wants to eat them. Subjects: | CYAC: Brothers and sisters—Fiction. | Twins—Fiction. | Adventure and adventurers—Fiction. | Monsters—Fiction. | Magic—Fiction. | Humorous stories. | BISAC: JUVENILE FICTION / Animals / Mythical. | JUVENILE FICTION / Humorous Stories. | JUVENILE FICTION / Action & Adventure / General. Classification: LCC PZ7.1.K509 At 2017 | DDC [Fic]—dc23 | LC record available at https://lccn.loc.gov/2016014964

Printed in the United States of America LB 0517
ISBN 978-1-4998-0394-5 (hc)
First Edition 10 9 8 7 6 5 4 3 2 1
ISBN 978-1-4998-0369-3 (pb)
First Edition 10 9 8 7 6 5 4 3 2
littlebeebooks.com
bonnierpublishingusa.com

ELLA AND OWEN

ATTACK OF THE STINKY FISH MONSTER!

by
Jaden Kent

little bee books

illustrated by
Iryna Bodnaruk

TABLE OF CONTENTS

1 ARE WE THERE YET?

"**W**e are *not* lost!" Ella said to her twin brother as they swam through the water.

"Right," Owen said. He gave his sister a blank look. "We just fell down a big hill, splashed into this lake, and don't know our way home."

"You say that like it's a bad thing," Ella replied. "Don't worry. My dragon sense will lead the way."

"Dragon sense? Ha!" Owen laughed.

"My dragon sense led us to Osgood the ogre and also the Cave of Aaaaah! Doom! and the Wizard Orlock Morlock, who cured your cold," Ella said proudly. "Just like I promised."

"You say that like it was a good thing!" Owen said. "Your dragon sense also got us into this mess and—whoa!" Owen flipped his tail out of the water. He looked behind himself nervously. "Something swam past me. Something BIG!"

"Don't be sil—*EEEEE!*" Ella screamed. "There *is* something in the water!" She began bobbing up and down.

"Maybe it's a friendly fish," Owen said hopefully. "A big friendly fish that wants to be friends because it's so friendly."

SPLASH! Suddenly, a huge Black Water Slime Eel jumped out from the water behind them. Its mouth snapped open. Giant fangs stuck out like tusks. Its angry scream sounded like an alarm. It was

"FLY AWAY!" Ella and Owen cried out at the same time.

Their dragon wings flapped as fast as wings can flap. They flew above the lake and—**_BONK!_** Ella and Owen crashed into each other.

SPLASH! They fell back into the water. The slime eel's back fin rose from the water like a sword. Its mouth opened, and it spit out the bones of a smaller fish. Huge fangs sparkled in the sun. Owen and Ella dove out of the way. The eel swam past, missing both of them.

"Grab the fin!" Ella yelled.

"No way!" Owen said. "That's crazy!"

Ella stretched her scaly arm and grabbed the slime eel's tail. "Follow me!"

"I'm too far away!" Owen yelled. "All I can grab is—" Owen grabbed Ella's tail.

The slime eel swam away fast, pulling Ella through the water. Owen hung on tightly.

"Stop tugging on my tail!" Ella yelled back to her brother.

"I'm trying to save you!" Owen shouted.

"That's so nice of you, but this is great! I'm a dragon cowgirl," Ella yelled. *"Yippee-ki-yay!"*

Then the slime eel lifted its tail out of the water and snapped it like a whip. Ella and Owen flew off the eel and headed toward the shore.

"*AAAAAH!*" they screamed as they sailed through the air.

"*OOOF!*" Air puffed from Ella's and Owen's stomachs as they crashed on the shore of the lake. The slime eel disappeared under the water, leaving only a ripple on the surface.

"See? That worked out great!" Ella said.

"Sure, if you like to eat sand," Owen said as he spit out a bunch of sand along with his forked tongue.

11

Ella shook the sand from between her scales. She pointed to a light in the distance. "Hey, Owen, is that the sprite we were chasing?"

"Do you mean the whole reason why we ended up in the lake in the first place? I don't care. I'm *not* going that way," Owen said. "I'm going the other way."

"Why?" asked Ella.

"Because every time I've chased that sprite, I've gotten lost or fallen down a hill or gotten thrown in a cage or almost gotten eaten! *This* way has to be better!" Owen pointed in the opposite direction of the light. He marched off, snout in the air. "This. Way." Then he tumbled down a hill.

"YAAAAAA!"

BOUNCE!
"OUCH!"

BOUNCE!
"OOOF!"

BOING!
"OUCH—OOOF!"

Ella leaned over the top of the hill and yelled down, "Owen! How's that other way working out?" She leaned too much, though. Then she tumbled down the hill as well. *"YAAAAAA!"*

BOUNCE!
"OUCH!"
BOUNCE!
"OOOF!"
BOING!
"OUCH—OOOF!"

She landed on top of Owen. "Thanks for breaking my fall. You're as soft as a bag of weaselbird feathers."

"Sure . . . feathers . . . *OOOF . . .*" Owen coughed, and Ella rolled off of him.

"Any idea where we are?" Ella asked.

"What? You don't know?" Owen replied. "Maybe I have *your* dragon sense. *I* know where we are!"

"How do you know that?" Ella asked

"Because we live over *there*!" Owen pointed toward a nearby path.

Ella saw that Fright Mountain was not that far away. She shrugged, acting as if she knew they were just minutes from their cave. "Race you!" Ella said.

"I'm halfway there already!" Owen flapped his wings and flew over the rocky trail.

Ella caught up quickly and passed her brother, but Owen stretched out his snout as far as it could go.

"Winner!" He skidded to a stop just as the front door to their cave opened up.

"Well, there you are!" their mother, Goldenrod, said.

"Mom! Dad!" Ella said.

"We're home!" Owen added.

"I'm glad to see the fresh air got rid of your cold," their mom said.

"Don't ask how," Owen mumbled. He stared at Ella, who smiled back.

"We're just on our way out," their father, Daryl, said.

"Where are you going?" Ella asked.

"If you're chasing a tree sprite, let me stop you right now. . . ." Owen said, still out of breath.

"Only a fool chases a tree sprite," Daryl said.

"Your father is such a romantic!" Goldenrod explained. "We're going out to scare the people in town."

Ella gave her parents a confused look. "You guys never do that kind of stuff anymore," she said.

A brief look of embarrassment crossed Daryl's face. "We know. It's not the *nicest* thing to do, but we're only looking to slightly scare the villagers," he said. "They *do* live right near Fright Mountain after all. . . ."

Ella and Owen both nodded, knowing how the villagers pretended that dragons didn't live nearby.

"Today is a special day for your mom. I'm taking her out as a special treat," Daryl explained.

"It's my birthday!" Goldenrod proudly said. "Isn't your father the sweetest?"

"Aww, you deserve it, my scaly beauty," Daryl said. He turned to Owen and Ella and whispered into their pointy ears. "You guys *did* remember that it's your mom's birthday, *right*?"

"Of c-c-course!" Ella stammered. "We'd *never* forget such an important day for Mom!"

"You betcha," Owen lied. "Yep. In fact, we got her the best gift ever!"

"Good!" Daryl whispered. "You can give it to her when we get back. She'll be *so* excited!"

"Are you ready, honey?" Goldenrod asked excitedly as she tapped her claws on the ground.

"Yep! Let's go!" said Daryl. "On three. One . . . two . . . *three!*"

Goldenrod and Daryl zoomed into the sky. Ella and Owen waved good-bye as their parents' long scaly tails disappeared into the clouds.

As soon as their parents were out of sight, Ella and Owen turned to each other and gasped. Their eyes went wide. Smoke puffed from their nostrils in a panic. *"I TOTALLY FORGOT TODAY WAS HER BIRTHDAY!"* they said at the same time.

"We've gotta get Mom a birthday gift!" Ella said.

"And fast!" Owen said. "Got any ideas?"

24

3
OFF TO SEE A WIZARD

"**O**kay—think!" Ella said to Owen as they walked through downtown Dragon Patch.

"I *am* thinking," Owen replied. "But what do you get your mom for her birthday when it's too late and you've forgotten?"

"I don't even have enough Dragon Ore to buy a new claw polisher," Ella said.

"Or a pearl-handled nose brush to clean out the dust from all the fire-breathing I did when I was sick," Owen said.

"Ewww," said Ella. "Let's try not to remember those sneezes, okay?"

Walking through Firebreather Square, they passed Fairy Frieda's Fairyland Diner, the Troll Market, the Minotaur Theatre, and Ye Olde Five Dwarves Repair Shoppe. A singing sword named Steve sang for vegetables, and an angry elf named Butterfingers offered to hit anyone on the head with his bashing mallet in return for a silver coin.

As they passed the Blind Bat's Baking Boutique, the smell of the baker's special claw and tomato cake gave Ella an idea.

"Cake!" Ella said. "We'll bake Mom a special cake! A newt cream cake with frosted toadstools."

"Great idea!" Owen agreed. "But I think a stinky fish cake with extra stinky fish on top and more stinky fish wrapped around the side would be even better."

"Newt cream!" Ella said.

"Stinky fish!" said Owen.

"Newt cream!"

"Stinky fish!"

They stopped arguing and stared at each other. Then both Ella and Owen said the same thing. *"TWO CAKES!"* they yelled.

Owen took off and ran inside Gorgon Goblin's Stinky Fish Emporium, the stinkiest fish shoppe in Dragon Patch (or so the sign claimed).

"Pee-YEW!" Owen said. "This place smells terrible! I love it!"

"Ugh! This place smells like an old dragon's ear wax." Ella sniffed the air again. "Mixed with the underarm hair from a swamp rat."

"Beautiful, isn't it?!" Owen took a deep sniff. "I could smell it all day long!"

"Are ye a'smellin' or a'buyin'?" asked Gorgon Goblin, the orange-and-tan shopkeeper.

Gorgon hopped on top of a large glass display case. Fish of different sizes and colors lined in ice were brought in from the top of Fright Mountain.

"We're buying, Mr. Gorgon Goblin, sir. A stinky fish, please," Owen requested. "Your stinkiest."

Gorgon reached into his display case. "You have chosen well, dragon boy," the fish seller said. He picked up a blue-and-orange grossfish and dropped it into a paper bag. He took a big whiff of the bag before sealing it. "Delicious! I keep several of these in my bathroom."

"That's too much information," Ella said. She turned to Owen. "Can we get my newt now?"

Owen paid for the grossfish with a piece of Dragon Ore. Gorgon licked it to make sure it was real and tossed it in the crate on the floor. "Have fun with the grossfish! They're even stinkier when they're cooked."

"This day just keeps getting better!" Owen said, smiling from ear to ear.

As they left Gorgon Goblin's Stinky Fish Emporium, Ella stopped and turned to her brother. "Umm—you need to walk behind me. Far, far behind me. Because *pee-YEW!*"

Ella waved her hand in front of her face as Owen walked behind her. He ignored his sister and instead tried to get a whiff of the grossfish inside the bag.

BA-BAM! Ella knocked on the door of the Olden Tyme Spells and Curses Depot. The door creaked open, and they stepped inside. A large puff of lime-green smoke filled the space in front of the twins.

33

"I am the great wizard," the great wizard said as he stepped out of the smoke. He wore a bright blue robe tied around his waist with a piece of rope. A ragged wizard's cap was on his head, covering a mass of gray hair. In his left hand, he held a bent wooden stick with a star tied to one end.

"The great wizard known by the ancient name of . . . Ken," the wizard said.

"Ken?" Ella asked. "Your name is *Ken*?"

"That doesn't sound like much of a wizard's name," Owen said.

"Blame my parents," the crusty old wizard replied.

Owen shook his head. "You need a cool wizardy name that's full of wizardness, like Wizard Zappo Wandacornium."

"And *you* dragony dragons should buy something or get out of my store," Ken snarled. "Before I curse you!"

Ella turned toward Owen and whispered, "More like Wizard Grumpo Grumpacornium."

Wizard Ken raised his magic wand. "Stop that whispering before I—whoa! What is that *horrible* smell? Have dragons never heard of soap and water?"

"It's the stink of my stinky fish," Owen said, holding his bag proudly in front of him.

Three trolls who walked through the door suddenly pinched their noses. "Ugh! This place smells terrible!" one troll said. "Let's go to Wally Wizard's Wizardly Wands and Pancakes!" said another troll as they stomped out of the store.

Ken stared at Ella and Owen. "Those were my best customers!" he said angrily.

"Don't worry. We're your new best customers," Ella said. "We'd like a newt."

"A newt?" Ken repeated. "A NEWT?!" The wizard pulled out his wand. "You stink up my store and send my customers running away for a measly newt?! I should turn *you* into a newt!"

Ken waved his wand in a circle. The star on top was covered in a swirl of magical energy. He swung the wand toward Ella.

"*BAM-A-KAZAM!*" Ken shouted, and then he whispered, "Oops."

The star on the top of the wand flew off the handle.

Owen ducked. The magical star sailed over his head and hit a cage on a shelf. The cage snapped open. Huge hairy spiders scampered out.

Ken ran across the room, jammed the star back onto his wand, and began casting more spells at Ella and Owen.

ZAP! ZAP! ZAPPITY-ZAP!

Magical bolts shot across the store. Ella and Owen ducked and dodged.

ZAPPITY-ZAP! ZAP!

The sparkly bolts hit cages and crates, busting them open. Eels slithered out. Three-winged bats flew across the store. Glass tanks of rainbow mice broke open. Bowls of ogre nail clippings emptied. Then Ella spotted a newt scurrying across the wooden floor.

She ran quickly to grab the newt,
careful to avoid Ken's zapping wand bolts.
"AH-HA!" Ella yelled. "Got one!" Ella picked
up the newt and tossed a piece of Dragon
Ore on the counter. "Let's go, Owen! We
have cakes to make!"

On the way out, Ella nearly tripped over the stinky fish bag. "Owen! You dropped your grossfish!" She looked around the store. No Owen. She grabbed the bag and ran out.

Outside the store, Ella looked all around and realized Owen was not with her. "Owen!" she yelled.

"I'm right here!" she heard Owen's voice say.

Ella looked in her hand. At the end of her claws was the newt she'd caught.

"It's me—Owen," the newt said. "I got hit by one of Ken's magic bolts. He turned me into a newt! *A newt!*" He sneezed a little newt sneeze. "And I'm allergic to myself!"

"Great," Ella said, "but can I use you in my birthday cake?"

"NO!" Owen the newt replied. Then he ate a bug. "Hmm. Not bad," he said.

42

5

TWO NEWTS AREN'T BETTER THAN ONE

"I can't believe my brother is a newt!" Ella said. "It was bad enough when you were a dragon, but now I'll be laughed out of Dragon Academy."

"Don't worry," Owen said. "There's a pixie shop across the street. Pixies have all kinds of magic junk. I'm sure they can help me," he said. They entered the Pixie Wishes Shoppe and were immediately greeted by a green glittery pixie.

"Greetings to you!" she said to Ella. "My name is Penelope Pepperpie. You can call me Penelope Pepperpie!" Then Penelope Pepperpie noticed the newt in Ella's paw. "Ah, I see you have brought me a beautiful, beautiful newt! He will make an excellent stew. How much do you want for him?"

"He's not for sale," Ella replied. "I want you to turn him back into my brother."

Penelope Pepperpie took a closer look at Owen and said, "Did you try Ken the wizard? He's very good with newt magic."

Owen's tail curled. "He's the one who turned me into a newt!"

"Can *you* change him back into a dragon?" Ella asked.

"*Oooh!* I love transformation spells! They are, like, *so* much fun to do!" Penelope Pepperpie clapped her little pixie hands.

"So you'll help us?" Ella asked.

"Of course! And it'll only cost ten Dragon Ores!" Penelope Pepperpie said.

"TEN?!" Ella gasped. "That's our whole allowance for a month! Isn't there something else we can do?"

"Well . . . I suppose you could do me one little, teeny-tiny, itty-bitty, not-big-at-all favor," Penelope Pepperpie began.

"What kind of little, teeny-tiny, itty-bitty, not-big-at-all favor?" Ella asked.

"Just say yes!" Owen insisted. "My skin is starting to dry out!"

"A delivery," Penelope Pepperpie said.

"Deal!" Owen snapped.

"Great! Please deliver this batch of fresh pixie dust to Wizard Ken." Penelope Pepperpie handed Ella a small sack of pixie dust. Magical sparkles swirled around the top of the sack.

"WHAT?!" cried Ella.

"You're joking, right?" Owen asked. "Did you not just listen to our story? He turned me into a *newt*! We can't go back there!"

"Well, *I* can't go there," Penelope Pepperpie said. "That grumpy old grump always tries to turn me into a toad, and I *must* make this delivery. Apparently two of his customers caused trouble and now his whole shop is a mess! He needs extra magic to clean it all up."

Owen quickly pictured his life as a newt and then shook the thought out of his head. "We'll do it," Owen said with a sigh.

"Okay, if you say so," Ella said, looking her brother in the eye. She took the bag of pixie dust from Penelope Pepperpie. "We're off to see the wizard," she said.

They walked down to the Olden Tyme Spells and Curses Depot. Owen sat on one of Ella's shoulders as they walked in and she tiptoed across the wooden floor. "So far, so good," she whispered to her tiny brother.

Until the floor creaked.

Then Wizard Ken rushed out from the back room. *"YOU!"* he shouted and waved his wand over his head. "I warned you!" Bolts and zaps shot across the room.

Moments later two newts ran out the front door of the Olden Tyme Spells and Curses Depot. Two newts named Owen and Ella.

"This is all *your* fault!" they shouted at each other.

6

PIXIE PROBLEMS

"**I** only promised to turn *one* of you back to normal if you made the delivery," Penelope Pepperpie explained. "But now that Ken has turned *both* of you into newts. . . ."

Ella and Owen were back at the pixie's shop. They were still newts, and Penelope Pepperpie was still a pixie. That had nothing to do with Ella and Owen still being newts, but it's always good to know who was still what when a grumpy wizard like Ken was zapping his wand at everyone.

49

"Then turn Ella back into a dragon," Owen said as he bravely puffed out his little newt chest.

"You're a very kind brother. You deserve a treat." Penelope Pepperpie reached into one of her cabinets and then fed Owen a beetle.

"Nah, I just can't wait to see how much trouble Ella's gonna get in when Mom and Dad find out that I'm a newt!" Owen laughed and gulped down the bug.

"Either we're both dragons or we're both newts, and I don't want to be a newt, so do you know what *that* means?" Ella asked.

"That I get all your bugs?" Owen scampered up the wall and onto the ceiling. "Hey! Being a newt is kinda cool!"

Penelope Pepperpie's wings fluttered like a green butterfly and flicked sparkly green glitter all over the store. "Okay, I'll turn you *both* back if you deliver another package for me." She put a smaller bag of pixie dust on the counter. "Bring this to Wizard Ken. He just ordered more."

"Tails and snails! We are *not* going back there!" Ella said. "Who knows what he'll turn us into this time?!"

"I hope it's *not* something with four heads!" Owen said.

Then . . . *PLOP!*

Ella heard something fall next to her.

In all the excitement, Owen accidentally fell off the ceiling and landed next to his sister. "That was close!" Owen said. "I almost squashed you, Sis!"

"We can't go back to Ken's shop. Is there anything else we can trade you to turn us back into dragons?" Ella asked.

"I'll give you all my ogre toenails," Owen offered.

"Nah," Penelope Pepperpie replied.

"Owen will give you all his dried bat wings," Ella offered.

"Nope," Penelope Pepperpie said.

"I'll give you my collection of fire snails," Owen offered.

"Uh-uh," Penelope Pepperpie replied, turning her head in disgust.

"Owen will give you his collection of lava worms," Ella offered.

"Why do you keep trying to give away my stuff?" Owen asked.

"Because it's not *my* stuff," Ella replied. "Seems like a no-brainer to me."

"Sorry, guys. I don't want any of those things. Pixies like stuff like rainbows and unicorns and rainbows made of unicorns and stinky fish cake and unicorns made of rainbows and—"

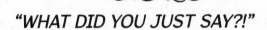

"WHAT DID YOU JUST SAY?!"
Owen and Ella both shouted.

"Unicorns made of rainbows?" Penelope Pepperpie asked.

"Before that!" Ella said.

"Stinky fish cake?" Penelope Pepperpie asked.

"Dragon tails! We'll make you a stinky fish cake if you turn us back into dragons!" Ella cheered.

"It's a deal, but only if you make it extra stinky!" Penelope Pepperpie clapped her tiny hands.

"If you wanna make stuff extra stinky, you've come to the right guy!" Owen proudly announced.

Penelope Pepperpie wiggled her ears and tossed a handful of pink glitter at Owen and Ella.

POOF! They were instantly covered in a sparkly cloud, and when the air cleared, Ella and Owen were dragons again!

"I'm so happy that I could hug you!" Ella cheered.

"Ugh! I'd rather be a newt!" Owen blew fire from his mouth to keep all possible hugs far away.

Penelope Pepperpie handed Ella a bag of pixie dust. "Please sprinkle a very, very, very little, teeny-tiny bit on the top of my stinky fish cake to make it glitter! Because, you know, pixies *love* glitter!"

The two dragons thanked the giggly little pixie and rushed toward home . . . but not before Owen ate one last beetle.

"The taste kinda grows on you," he said. He grabbed the bag with the grossfish inside and followed his sister out the door.

"**I**'ve got the slime!" Ella called out.

"I've got the salamander eggs!" Owen called back.

"Here's the worm powder!" Ella added.

"I need more toad warts!" Owen said.

Back at their cave, Ella and Owen rushed to make two stinky fish cakes—one for their mom and one for Penelope Pepperpie.

"And last but not least, some grossfish
on top!" Owen said, proud of their work.

Ella whipped out the bag of pixie dust
and sprinkled some onto the second cake.
"There! A very, very, very little, teeny-tiny
bit just like Penelope Pepperpie said."

"Don't we want to make it special for Penelope Pepperpie? She *did* turn us back into dragons," Owen said. He took the bag of pixie dust from his sister and dumped the whole thing onto the cake. "If a very, very, very little, teeny-tiny bit will make the cake glitter, the whole bag should make it light up like fireworks!"

BOOM! The cake exploded and the kitchen turned into a cloud of pixie dust and cake pieces. The explosion had ruined both cakes, and covered Ella and Owen in bits and pieces of cake.

"Nice going, Bro," Ella said. She brushed some cake pieces off her wings. "Got any more bright ideas in that scaly head of yours?"

"Yes," Owen replied, staring at what used to be their cakes. *"RUN!"* he yelled.

A loud roar filled the room!

The huge amount of pixie dust had turned the stinky fish into a giant stinky fish monster . . . and it was hungry! It had blue-and-orange fish scales, two short legs, and a huge mouth, big enough to swallow Ella and Owen in one fishy gulp! Worst of all was its odor! *Pee-yew!* It smelled worse than Owen after a week without a bath!

Ella and Owen flew from their cave as quickly as their little wings could carry them. The stinky fish monster stomped after them, its fishy mouth chomping at their tails.

"That thing's trying to eat us!" Owen shouted.

"It's only fair," Ella said as they flew for their lives. "We were going to eat him first, but I have a plan! We have to get that stinky fish monster to Wizard Ken!"

"Back to the wizard?!" Owen gasped. "You're worse than that pixie Pepperpie Pooppip Pipeapoo—or whatever her name is! That's the kinda plan a bridge troll would make up!"

"BLAAAAAARG!" The stinky fish monster blaaaaaarged and covered Owen in slimy fish monster slobber.

"On second thought, I love your idea!" Owen said, wiping off his wings. "Let's go!"

They flew toward downtown Dragon Patch and . . . watched as the stinky fish monster ran the other way toward the lake.

"It's getting away!" Ella panicked.

"It's not getting away—*we're* getting away!" Owen corrected.

"Quick! Fly after him! He has to chase us!" Ella said.

"What? Did you breathe fire on your little brain or something?" Owen couldn't believe it. "Why would we do that?!"

"Because it's part of the *plan*!" Ella replied.

"Then let's make up a *new* plan where the fish monster that's *trying* to eat us *doesn't* eat us because it disappeared into a lake instead!" Owen shouted.

Ella didn't answer. She was too busy shouting at the stinky fish monster. "Hey, stinky fish monster! Come eat my brother!"

"What? Why me?" Owen complained.

"If you don't want to get eaten, make up your own plan next time," Ella said.

The stinky fish monster stopped. It turned and glared at Owen with its scary yellow eyes.

"Look at m-m-me. So t-t-tasty," Owen stammered and then licked his arm. "Mmm-mmm g-g-good."

The stinky fish monster licked its fat pink lips with a gooey purple tongue and then leaped at Owen.

"AAAAAAAH!" Owen screamed and flew away with Ella.

The stinky fish monster roared and chased them down the path toward Wizard Ken's shop.

GLARG! BLARG! PLARG!

The stinky fish monster glarged, blarged, and plarged as it stomped through the narrow streets of downtown Dragon Patch, trying to catch its dinner, which just happened to be named Owen and Ella.

"You got yourself a mighty stinky pet!" a fairy named Dewdrop said to Ella and Owen.

"It's not our pet!" Ella blurted out as they flew past.

The stinky fish monster roared at Dewdrop. She quickly flew into Ye Olde Five Dwarves Repair Shoppe and hid in a dwarf's beard.

The creatures of downtown Dragon Patch screamed and raced to safety. Trolls hid under bridges, witches flew away on brooms, and elves climbed trees to escape.

"Sorry, folks! Show's over!" Steve the singing sword yelped and hopped away on his hilt the moment he saw the stinky fish monster.

"Where is this monster?! I'll bash him back to Stinky Swamp!" Butterfingers the angry elf shouted and waved his bashing mallet over his head.

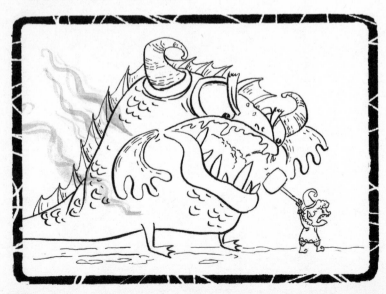

GULP! The stinky fish monster swallowed Butterfingers's bashing mallet in one gulp. He would've swallowed Butterfingers in one gulp as well if the elf hadn't run away screaming.

"Hey! Over here!" Ella yelled to the stinky fish monster so he'd chase them again.

The stinky fish monster jumped at them and grabbed Ella's tail in its mouth.

"OOOOOOO-WEEEEEEN!" she yelled.

"Is this part of your plan, too?" Owen gasped as he struggled to pull her free.

"PULL!" Ella shouted.

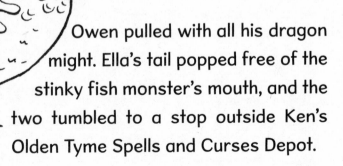

Owen pulled with all his dragon might. Ella's tail popped free of the stinky fish monster's mouth, and the two tumbled to a stop outside Ken's Olden Tyme Spells and Curses Depot.

"Perfect! We're here!" Ella said.

"Ugh! What's that smell?" Ken stormed from his shop. "You two again?" he shouted the moment he saw Owen and Ella in a heap on the ground. "This time I'm gonna turn you two pests into Pink-Bottomed Burping Bugs!"

"I bet you're not a good enough wizard to turn us into a glittery stinking fish cake!" Ella said.

A furious Ken whipped out his wand. "I could do that with my eyes closed!"

The stinky fish monster, which was right next to Owen, opened its huge mouth to swallow the dragons.

"Less talking, more wand zapping!" Owen yelped.

ZAP! A bolt of magic shot from Ken's wand. Ella flapped her wings and barely avoided the blast.

BLAMMO! It was a direct hit to the stinky fish monster. It went from being a horrible creature trying to eat Ella and Owen to a delicious glittery dessert, but it was still stinky.

"You won't dodge me this time!" Ken aimed his wand at Ella and Owen.

There was no escape, so the two dragons did what any brother and sister would do before a grumpy wizard turned them into a glittery stinking fish cake. They pointed a finger at each other and shouted . . .

"IT'S ALL HER FAULT!"
"IT'S ALL HIS FAULT!"

Then, just as it looked like Ella and Owen might be turned into stinky desserts themselves, the downtown Dragon Patch townsfolk rushed over and lifted Ken into the air.

"You saved the town!" a dwarf with a red beard down to his feet yelled to Ken.

"Three cheers for Wizard Zappo Wandacornium!" Owen cried out.

"My name is Ken!" Ken shouted, but no one cared.

"Wizard Zappo Wandacornium! Wizard Zappo Wandacornium! Wizard Zappo Wandacornium!" the crowd cheered.

"Stop calling me that! My name is *KEN*!" Ken protested.

"Let's hear it for Wizard Grumpo Grumpacornium!" Ella yelled.

"Hooray for Wizard Grumpo Grumpacornium!" ogres, elves, gnomes, fairies, and trolls cheered as they carried Ken down the street. "Wizard Grumpo Grumpacornium! Wizard Grumpo Grumpacornium! Wizard Grumpo Grumpacornium!"

Ella grabbed the cake. "Come on! Mom and Dad will be home any minute!"

"Oh! Is that my stinky fish cake? I love it!" Penelope Pepperpie squealed as she fluttered over.

"But we need it for—" Owen started to say.

"Love it! Love it! Love it!" Penelope Pepperpie continued.

"We have to give it to—" Ella said.

"It's perfect with a capital *Pixie*! Thanks for making it for me. Our deal is done!" Penelope Pepperpie grabbed the cake from Ella, and she disappeared in a cloud of purple pixie dust.

"Aw, dragon scales!" Ella growled. "She took our only cake! We needed it to give to Mom!"

"I know! And she didn't even ask me if I wanted a slice!" Owen grumbled.

Ella and Owen flew back to their cave as fast as they could. They wiped down the kitchen so there were no signs of exploded cake. When the last spot was cleaned, Ella turned to her brother with wide eyes. "We've got no cake for Mom and no time to get anything!" she said. She looked around nervously, searching for *something* to give their mom.

"We don't need a cake. I've got a backup plan!" Owen whipped out his backup plan and proudly showed it to Ella. "Go ahead," he said. "You can thank me now."

"You're kidding, right? That's just a pinecone with mustard on top," Ella said, squinting at the object in Owen's hand.

"Don't knock it until you try it!" Owen took a bite and then spit it out. "*Blech!* Okay, knock it all you want. That thing tastes *terrible!*"

"It's been *so* long since we scared villagers like that. . . ." someone said just outside their cave.

"MOM!" Ella and Owen shouted.

"Yeah . . . good times," they heard someone else say.

"DAD!" Ella and Owen shouted. Again.

"Hey, kids! How's it flapping?" their dad asked as he flew into the cave with their mom. "Is there anything you want to say to your mom?"

"There sure is!" Ella said and whipped out Owen's pinecone with mustard—with a bite taken out of it. "Happy birthday, Mom! We love you! Gotta go!"

"Is that a pinecone with mustard on top?" their mom asked.

"Don't knock it until you try it." Ella chuckled.

"Very funny, kids," their dad said.

Ella and Owen looked at each other guiltily. Ella felt terrible. Owen felt miserable. They *wanted* to give their mom a present on her special day.

"We went to get a present in downtown Dragon Patch, but Wizard Zappo Wandacornium didn't like my stinky fish, so he turned me into a newt!" Owen started babbling.

"And Penelope Pepperpie wouldn't turn him back unless we made a delivery to Grumpo Grumpacornium, but he turned me into a newt, too!" Ella rambled.

"And Pickadoo Porcupine wanted us to make a second delivery, but we traded a stinky cake that we didn't have to Penelope, but I poured too much pixie dust!" Owen was babbling even faster.

"And the fish tried to eat us because we wanted to eat him. Then Grumpo Grumpacornium zapped him, and then Peter Piper Picked a Peck of Pickled Peppers took the cake. Then Owen made a pinecone with mustard!" Ella rambled even faster than her brother.

"Did you get *any* of that?" their dad whispered to their mom.

"Of course," their mom began. "Cranky old Wizard Ken turned them into newts. Penelope Pepperpie the pixie offered to turn them back in exchange for a stinky fish cake, but Owen used too much pixie dust—you know how much pixies *love* glitter—and the fish turned into a monster and tried to eat them. Then Ella came up with a plan—very clever, dear—to lead the monster to Dragon Patch where they tricked Ken into turning it into a stinky fish cake. Unfortunately, Penelope Pepperpie thought it was a cake for her and took it. So Owen made a pinecone covered in mustard—I love your creativity, honey—to give to me instead."

Their dad stared at their mom in shock.

"What?" their mom asked. "It's a mother's *job* to know what her kids are talking about."

"We're sorry we messed up your birthday, Mom." Ella sighed.

"Messed it up? You got me the best present ever!" their mom said.

"See! I told you she'd like the pinecone!" Owen said to Ella.

"No, I mean annoying that cranky, old Wizard Ken!" Their mom laughed. "He's *always* so rude to me! I've wanted to singe that wrinkled old grouch's beard whiskers for years! But your father won't let me."

"The last thing we need is everyone showing up at our cave with torches and pitchforks, dear," their dad began. "Although . . . your mom's right. Ruffling that nincompoop's pointy hat *is* a pretty good gift. But I'd rather have a stinky fish cake."

"We're on it, Dad! We know a great recipe—sort of—and can make you one!" Ella said.

"No way. I've had enough of downtown Dragon Patch for today—and the rest of my life." Owen snorted. "I've got a stack of books just begging me to read them!"

"We don't need to *buy* a stinky fish in downtown Dragon Patch," Ella explained. "We can go to Terror Swamp and catch one!"

"T-t-terror Swamp?!" Owen stammered. "Who names these places?"

"Maybe Ken's parents," Ella replied. "They're not very good with names, after all. Come on, Bro!"

Ella grabbed a fishing pole and flew from the cave.

"Good-bye, books. I promise to come back and read you . . . as long as nothing in Terror Swamp eats me first." Owen sighed and reluctantly followed his sister.

Read on for a sneak peek from the third
book in the Ella and Owen series!

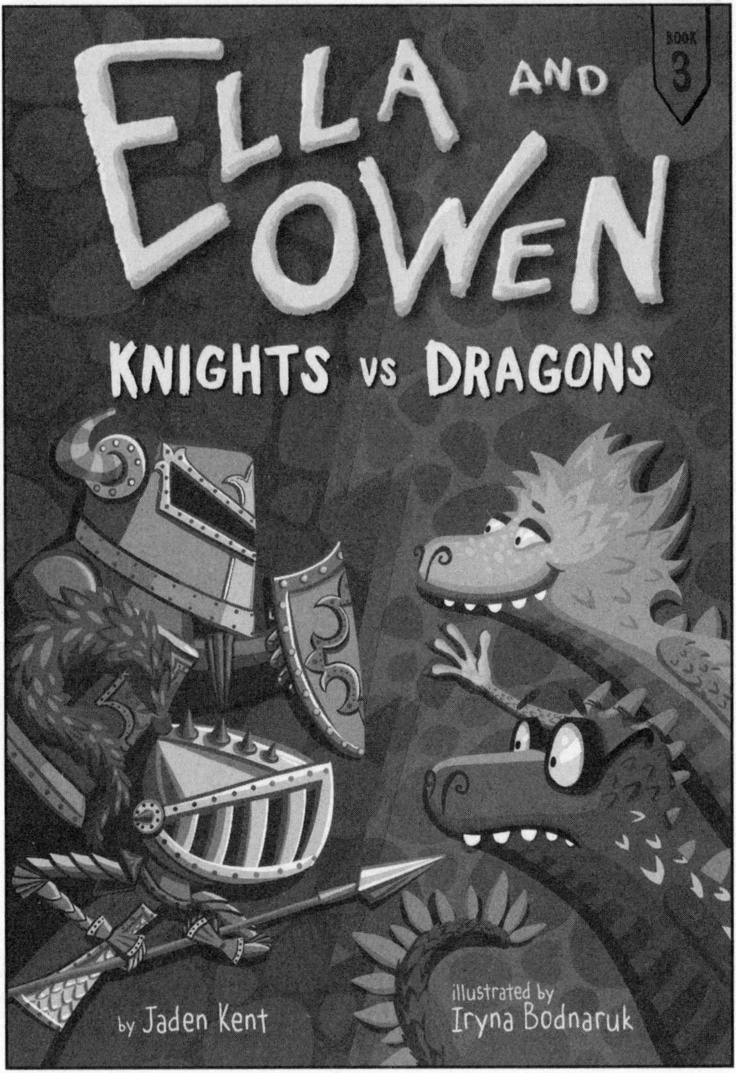
BOOK
3
ELLA AND OWEN
KNIGHTS VS DRAGONS
by Jaden Kent
illustrated by
Iryna Bodnaruk

"If something in Terror Swamp tries to eat me, I'm totally blaming you," Owen said.

"Me?" his sister Ella replied.

"Yes, you!! Going to Terror Swamp was your idea, not mine."

"We can't disappoint Dad," Ella said. "He's expecting a stinky fish, and we're going to catch it for him." The fishing pole over her shoulder swung back and forth as her clawed feet trampled through the forest.

The two dragons had left their home in Dragon Patch that morning with a promise to catch a stinky fish for their father. Unfortunately, as all dragons know, the best stinky fish swim in the muddy waters of Terror Swamp.

"Are you sure this is the way to our doom, I mean, Terror Swamp?" Owen asked.

"It's a shortcut I've heard of," Ella said. "This path through the forest takes us to the other side of Fright Mountain."

"What?! You mean the wrong side of Fright Mountain! W-where the k-knights live?!" Owen fearfully exclaimed.

"I've read the books and the scrolls about those knights in that castle, and I've listened to the awful stories from Uncle Scales and Great-Great-Grandmother Clawfoot. Knights hate dragons as much as trolls hate baths." Owen's wings nervously fluttered.

"Don't you wanna see a real castle and a live knight?!" Ella asked.

"Why would I want to meet anything that wants to turn my beautiful scaly skin into a pair of dragon boots?!" Owen asked. "I don't want to be boots, or shoes, or sandals, or—"

"Would it be better if they wanted to turn you into a hat?" Ella joked.

"There is nothing you can say to change my mind!" Owen huffed. "There's no way I'm going to that castle with you! No way!"

"Well, then I guess you'll just have to go back home . . . all by yourself,"

Ella said. "Back through the Fear Forest . . . the Field of Dread . . . and the Sands of Suffering . . . but you know best." Her wings fluttered. "Ta-ta, little brother." She flew off and headed toward the castle. Owen looked around, filled with fear.

"Okay, there's no way you're going to that castle without me!" Owen's wings fluttered faster and he took off after his sister.

The two dragons flew through the sky and into the clouds. In just a few minutes, the clouds disappeared, and before them was the castle of the knights who hate dragons.

The castle was made of stone blocks, with a high tower at each corner and a large wooden door.

"It's beautiful!" Owen cried out. "Just like in my books! Except for the big banner!"

Across the door was a big banner.

The two dragons landed behind a thick row of bushes near the castle. Owen pushed the branches apart and peeked out.

"Look at all the people in the village," Ella said. "They're singing. It's some kind of festival."

"Check out the banner over the castle door." Owen pointed. "This is our kind of party!"

The banner had only two handwritten words splattered on it: DRAGON DAY!

"I told you the knights weren't so bad," Ella said. "They celebrate dragons."

"Uh, Ella, what's that ugly thing under the banner?" Owen said.

There was a large bag of straw hanging from a rope. Four wooden poles stuck out from the bag that looked a little like arms and legs. A pumpkin was tied to one end of the bag. Two eyes and a jagged mouth had been carved out of it.

"I think that's supposed to be a dragon," Ella replied.

Four knights gathered around the "dragon." Villagers happily danced and stuffed themselves with meat and cheese and bread. An old bard with a long gray beard sat with his mandolin, but didn't play it. "Happy Dragon Day!" the crowd roared. "Happy Dragon Day!"

Owen smiled. "Maybe these humans aren't so bad after all if they have a holiday named after dragons!"

"Smash the dragon!" one of the knights shouted.

The villagers stopped dancing. They picked up tomatoes and apples from the festival tables and threw them at the bag of straw. The bard even used his mandolin to bash the fake dragon a few times.

"Happy Dragon Day," he sang.

"Wow," Ella said as they watched from their hiding place. "Worst holiday ever."